The Bears

of the Evergreen

Forest

Basil and Brenda Go for a Stroll

AuthorHouse™ UK
1663 Liberty Drive
Bloomington, IN 47403 USA
www.authorhouse.co.uk
Phone: 0800 047 8203 (Domestic TFN)
+44 1908 723714 (International)

Because of the dynamic nature of the Internet, any web addresses or links contained in this book may have changed since publication and may no longer be valid. The views expressed in this work are solely those of the author and do not necessarily reflect the views of the publisher, and the publisher hereby disclaims any responsibility for them.

Any people depicted in stock imagery provided by Getty Images are models, and such images are being used for illustrative purposes only. Certain stock imagery © Getty Images.

This book is printed on acid-free paper.

ISBN: 978-1-7283-9760-3 (sc)
ISBN: 978-1-7283-9761-0 (e)

Print information available on the last page.

Published by AuthorHouse 02/06/2020

authorHOUSE®

The Bears

of the Evergreen

Forest

Basil and Brenda Go for a Stroll

HAZEL THOMPSON

Basil sat by his favourite tree in the Evergreen Forest. He was listening to the chattering birds, watching the fish in the lake and the ants going about their work. He suddenly had an idea. He decided to ask his sister Brenda whether she wanted to walk into the village and have a picnic.

Basil knocked on Brenda's door and waited for an answer. After waiting for a little time with no luck, he knocked on the door again. He could hear something going on inside and knew that Brenda was in there so he knocked a little louder.

Finally the door opened and there was Brenda. Brenda said 'Hello' and invited Basil to come in. Basil asked Brenda what she had been doing. He said it was frustrating when you knocked on a door and no-one answered. 'Oh sorry Basil', said Brenda, 'I didn't hear you. I was clearing out my cupboard. How long had you been waiting?' 'Oh not too long. I was wondering if you wanted to take a walk into the village. It is such a lovely day and it would be such a shame to waste it.'

'Wonderful idea Basil! I have some letters to post. I can finish tidying this later'. They set off along the lane towards the Post Office.

As they started to walk along the lane, Brenda asked Basil if he had seen their friends, Pip and Tara recently. 'Yes' replied Basil. 'I saw them on the lake yesterday. They had borrowed Mr. Bertrand's lily boat and one of Mrs. Potter's sheets to make a sail. I was watching them from the riverbank. It was very funny because the wind blew so hard that the boat went right over and they fell out and got wet.' Basil and Brenda started laughing.

Just then the bear's little friend Polly called from a tree she was sitting in. 'Yes, that was funny. I was in my nest in the big birch tree and saw the whole thing. Oh look, here they come now', said Polly, as Pip and Tara ran up the lane towards the bears.

'What's so funny?', asked Pip, 'what are you laughing at?'.

'I was just telling Brenda about your sailing trip on the lake yesterday', said Basil. 'Oh yes that was funny', laughed Tara. 'Where are you heading? Anywhere nice?'

'We are going to the village to post some letters', said Brenda. 'Then we are going to have a picnic by the lake'.

'Well, have fun', replied Polly, and she flew back to her nest to look after her little babies.

Basil asked Pip and Tara if they would like to join him and Brenda for the picnic later. Pip and Tara said they would love to and would bring some of their mother's elderflower cordial.

The LAKE

The FOREST

Basil and Brenda arrived in the village. They waved to their friends along the road. As they entered the Post Office, Mrs Tilley the wise old owl who ran the store called her own greeting to them. 'Basil, Brenda, lovely to see you both, what brings you here today?' she said. 'Oh I see you have more letters Brenda'. 'Yes Mrs. Tilley, to my cousins in the West Woods' replied Brenda handing over two small brown envelopes and a couple of coins to pay for postage.

Mrs Tilley took the envelopes, stamped them and put them in the bag so the Postie could deliver them. 'Well it is a lovely day, enjoy your walk home' said Mrs Tilley as the Bears left the post office to go to the bun shop. 'Let's buy some bread and jam for the picnic', said Basil. When they had bought the bread and jam they went to meet Pip and Tara.

They arrived at the clearing and sat beneath a large beech tree. Just then, Pip and Tara ran up. The friends shared all the food and drink which were very yummy.

After the picnic they played hide and seek all around the clearing. By sunset they were all exhausted, so they all went to the big rock near their home tree to watch the sun go down.

They fell asleep under the Evergreen Forest's starry night sky.

THE END

ACTIVITIES

Have fun colouring in the picture below

ACTIVITIES

1. HIDE AND SEEK – Can you spot Basil, Pip and Tara hiding from Brenda in the clearing?

2. What different animals can you see in the Village picture?

3. How many birds, ants and fish can you see in the lake picture?

Printed in the United States
By Bookmasters